This book features fun, new words to the song.

Louis Weber, C.E.O.
Publications International, Ltd.
7373 North Cicero Avenue
Lincolnwood, Illinois 60646

Manufactured in the U.S.A.

ISBN: 0-7853-0983-7

JACK AND JILL

ILLUSTRATED BY
TRICIA ZIMIC

Publications International, Ltd.

Jack and Jill went up the hill
    To fetch a pail of water.

Jack fell down and broke his crown,
    And Jill came tumbling after.

Jack and Jill went down the street
Soon after this disaster.

Jill slid on a banana peel,
And Jack slipped even faster.

Jack and Jill slipped and slid
  Into a big mud puddle.

He grabbed her foot, she pulled his tail;
  They were a muddy huddle.

Jack and Jill went to the woods
    To look for their friend Tom Cat.

They lost their way and had to stay
    With Sam and Suzy Muskrat.

Jack and Jill went to the lake
    To swim and fish all day.

They splashed so much, they later learned,
    They scared the fish away.

Jack and Jill went to their school
  To learn the alphabet.

Jack liked to play and didn't stay,
  But Jill was teacher's pet.

Jack and Jill went to the park
　　To play ball with the home team.

Jack hit four, Jill slammed two more,
　　And everyone had ice cream.

Jack and Jill walked to the store
   To buy cornmeal and flour.
They told their mom that they'd be home
   In less than half an hour.

Jack and Jill invited friends
  To catch fireflies in jars.
The field was filled with sparkling lights;
  The sky sparkled with stars.

Jack and Jill climbed into bed;
    Their mother lit a night-light.

She kissed them both and tucked them in
    And said, "Good night and sleep tight."